To Tom and Kathy who are never bored. (Well hardly ever!)

Published by **Doubleday,** a division of Bantam Doubleday Dell Publishing Group, Inc.,
666 Fifth Avenue, New York, New York 10103. **Doubleday** and the portrayal of an anchor with a
dolphin are trademarks of Doubleday, a division of Bantam Doubleday Dell Publishing Group, Inc.

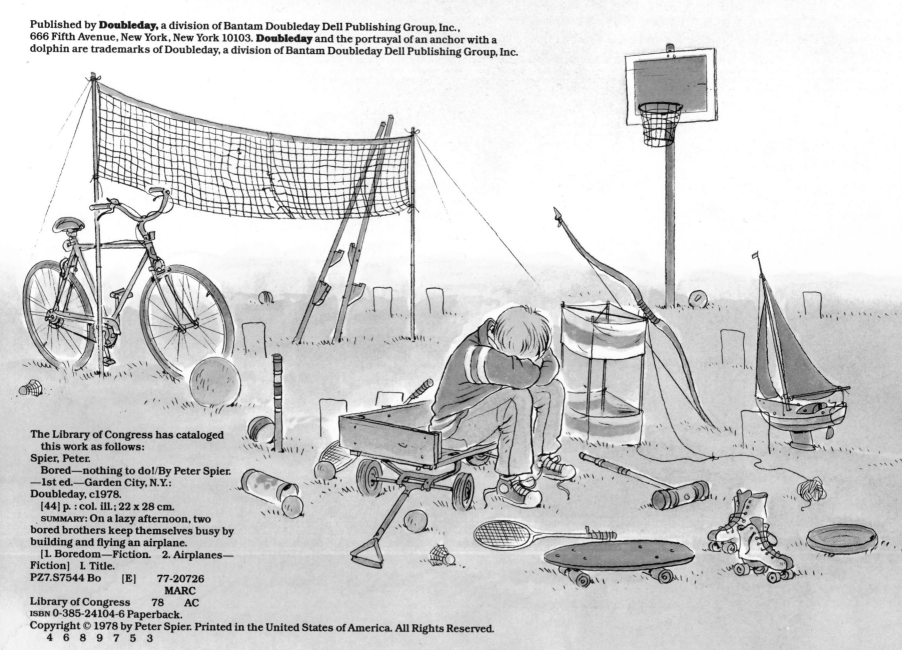

The Library of Congress has cataloged
   this work as follows:
Spier, Peter.
    Bored—nothing to do!/By Peter Spier.
—1st ed.—Garden City, N.Y.:
Doubleday, c1978.
    [44] p. : col. ill.; 22 x 28 cm.
    SUMMARY: On a lazy afternoon, two
bored brothers keep themselves busy by
building and flying an airplane.
    [1. Boredom—Fiction. 2. Airplanes—
Fiction] I. Title.
PZ7.S7544 Bo   [E]   77-20726
                    MARC
Library of Congress   78   AC
ISBN 0-385-24104-6 Paperback.

BORED–NOTHING TO DO!

by *Peter Spier*

Doubleday

NEW YORK   LONDON   TORONTO   SYDNEY   AUCKLAND

"Go do something. I was never bored at your age!"

"Let's make something."   **"What?"**

But how?

So that's how it works.

They need wheels...and wood...and seats...and nails...

and paint...and glue...and cloth...and hinges...and rope...

and windshields...and screws...

You need a lot of stuff to build an airplane.

Hard work!

"Need wire."

That is easy.

How about that?

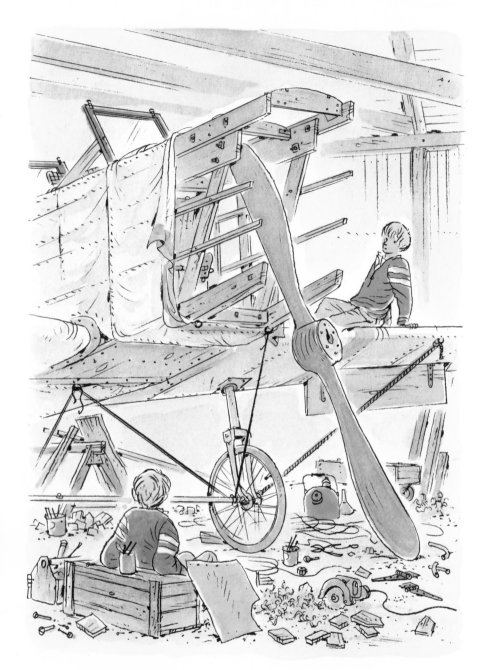

A plane needs an engine.

Too small.

Too heavy.

Just right!

Messy job. Tiring.

"To make it run, turn the key."

Noisy!...Scary!...But it works.

It flies...

It really flies.

Great plane!

TV doesn't work.
Call a repair man.

Phone doesn't work.
Go get a repair man,
and the telephone company.

Car will not start.

(Of course not!)

"Where are my sheets?"

"Look at the baby carriage...

and what happened to the bicycles?"

"What happened to our fence?"

"…and to my clothesline?"

"…and to the garden furniture?"

"Nothing works!" (Small wonder!)
"Where is everything?" "Where are the boys?"

"Come down immediately!!"

"I think they are angry."   "May as well go down."

Nice landing.

A good spanking (and a kiss).

"Put it all back where it belongs!"

The engine.

The gas tank.

The windows.

The chairs.

The rope.

The sheets (a little bit torn).

The wire.

The paint...but how?

The wheels.

The fence.

The wood.

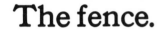

The tools.

Everything.

Sent to their room. Early!

"Some boys." "Clever, too!"

Bored—nothing to do!